For Anna with thanks – and love ~J.H.

To my boys with love ~B.G.

First published 2002 by Walker Books Ltd
87 Vauxhall Walk, London SE11 5HJ

This edition published 2003

10 9 8 7 6 5 4 3 2 1

Text © 2002 Judy Hindley
Illustrations © 2002 Brita Granström

The right of Judy Hindley and Brita Granström
to be identified as author and illustrator respectively
of this work has been asserted by them in accordance
with the Copyright, Designs and Patents Act 1988

This book has been typeset in Gararond

Printed in Italy

British Library Cataloguing in Publication Data:
a catalogue record for this book is available
from the British Library

ISBN 0-7445-9807-9

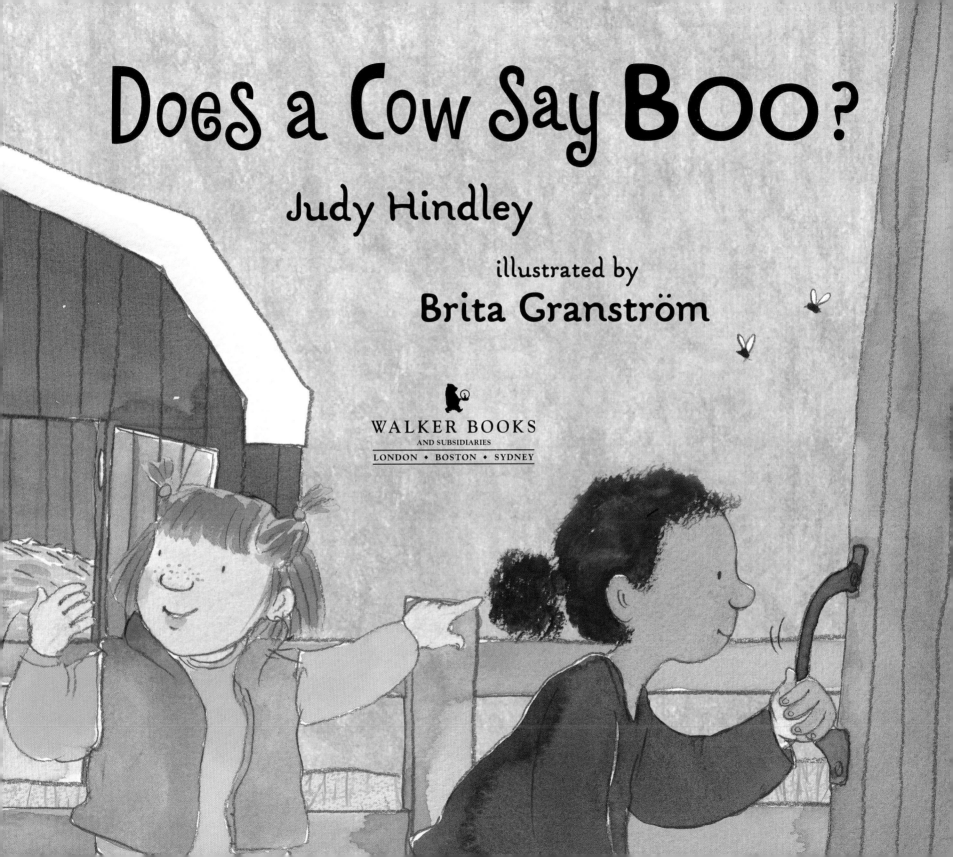

Does a Cow Say Boo?

Judy Hindley

illustrated by
Brita Granström

WALKER BOOKS
AND SUBSIDIARIES
LONDON • BOSTON • SYDNEY

moo!

That's what a cow says — and you can, too.

So who says **BOO**?

Does a pig say **BOO?**
Oh, no!

A pig says **oink!**

But who says **BOO**?
Does a dog say **BOO**?

Oh dear, no!
What does a dog say?

Well then, does a cat say **BOO**?
Don't be silly!
A cat says **mew!**
And a cat says **meow!**

And a cat goes *purrrr*
when you stroke
her fur.

So who, who,
who says **BOO**?

Does an owl say **BOO**?
No, no, no!
An owl says
whoo —
tu-whit
tu-whoo!

And down below
a mouse goes
squeak!
A horse says
neigh!

And way up high on the hen house roof
the rooster throws back his head
to crow...

How does he go?

What a hullabaloo!

A duck says **quack,**

a bird says **tweet,**

a hen says **cluck**

and her chicks say **cheep,**

a bee goes **buzz,**

a sheep says **baa ...**

though some little

creatures say nothing at all.

So isn't there anyone who says **BOO**?

Hide your eyes and tell me who.

What do you say now?

You say ...